Arthur's Really Helpful WORKBOOKS

ABC Reach for the Stars!

Marc Brown

Random House 🏠 **New York**

Copyright © 1998 by Marc Brown.
All rights reserved under International and Pan-American Copyright Conventions.
Published in the United States by Random House, Inc., New York, and simultaneously in Canada
by Random House of Canada Limited, Toronto.
ISBN 0-679-89284-2

Printed in the United States of America   10 9 8 7 6 5 4 3 2 1

www.randomhouse.com/kids

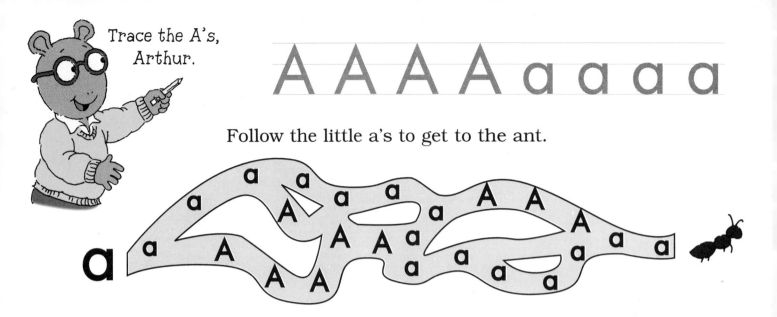

Trace the A's, Arthur.

AAAAaaaa

Follow the little a's to get to the ant.

Draw a red circle around the things that start with the letter A.

ASTRONAUTS, ALL!

ELIZA

Can you find the sticker of the A word and stick it where it belongs?

B B B B b b b b

Now trace the B's, D.W.

Draw a black line beneath the things that do not begin with B.

Draw a blue circle around the small b's.

B   B   B   b   B   B   b   b   B   B   b   B

Find the B–word sticker and put it where it belongs.
(Hint: It's black and blue, and rectangular, too!)

Trace the C's, then make them yourself.

C C C   C C C

Draw a green ring around the thing that begins with C.

Color in the thing that begins with C.

COZY CAPSULE

STAR WORLD

COMICS

Find some C-word stickers so the astronauts can have a sweet snack or two...or more!

D D D D

d d d d

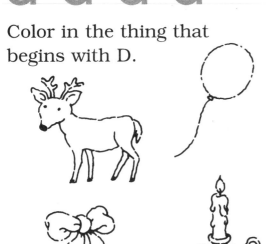

Color in the thing that begins with D.

Trace the big and little D's, then make them yourself.

Draw a line to match the big D to the little d.

A	c
C	d
D	a
B	b

DOG STARS

Find the D–word sticker that will help the Dog Stars get the beat.

E E E E e e e e

Color in the thing that begins with E.

Draw a line under the big E's. Draw a circle around the little e's.

Electric eels are teeny next to elephants.

THE EGG MAN

Only eggs? Find the E sticker to stick here and
relieve this eggs-quisite monotony.

F F F F   f f f f

Draw a line beneath the pictures of the objects that do not begin with F.

Find Arthur and D.W. some fantastic F gifts to give to the alien.

G G G   g g g

Color the G word green.

Draw a line to match
the big G with the little g.

C	e
D	d
B	c
G	b
E	g

GALACTIC GREENHOUSE

This garden could use a few G animals, don't you think?

H H H   h h h

Draw a red circle around the
thing that begins with H.

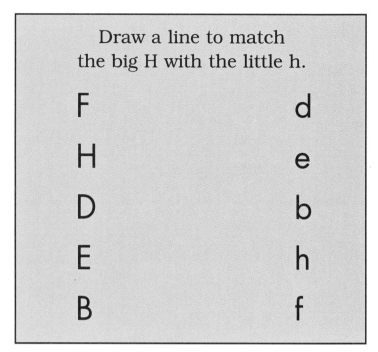

Draw a line to match
the big H with the little h.

F	d
H	e
D	b
E	h
B	f

PLANET OF THE HUGE HAIRY HAMSTERS

Haven't you heard? Hamsters like music!
Find two musical instruments that begin with the letter H.

I I I I   i i i i

Can you dot the little i's in this interesting sentence?

Ice cream is not icky, is it?

Draw a line beneath the words that do not begin with the letter I.

igloo   **ice cream**   **soda can**

ICE CREAM MOUNTAIN

Find a sticker of an I word that is not cold.

J J J J   j j j j

Draw a circle around the picture of the J word.

Draw a line to match the big J to the little j.

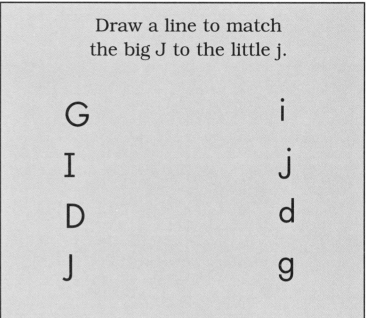

G   i

I   j

D   d

J   g

JUMPING JUPITER!

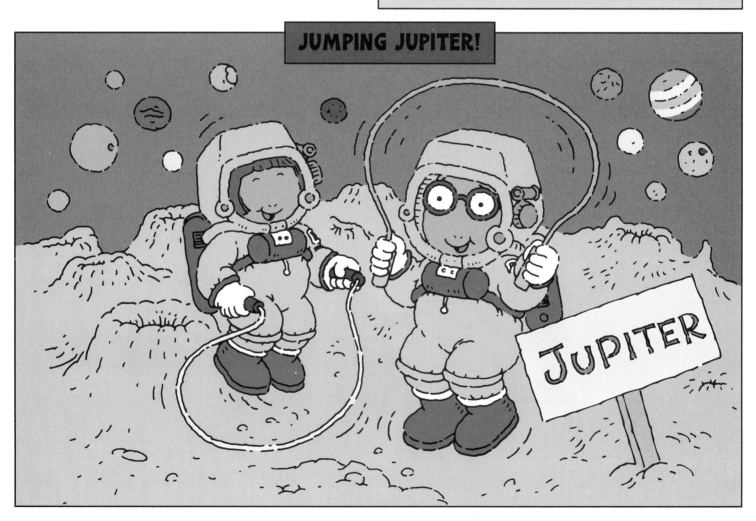

JUPITER

What other toys can they play with on Jupiter?

K K K K   k k k

Color in the thing that begins with K.

Draw a line under the big K's.

k k K K k K k k K K k K

GO FLY A KITE!

Find the K–word sticker that will make D.W. a regular Ben Franklin.

LLLL IIII

Draw a line beneath the big L's in the sentence below. Draw a circle around the little l's.

Lions like to lick large lunchboxes.

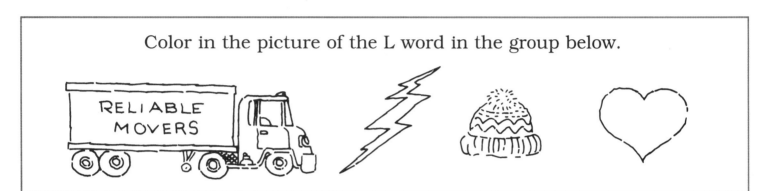

Color in the picture of the L word in the group below.

LET'S GO TO THE LIBRARY!

Find the sticker of the object that begins with L.
(Hint: They don't really need one in this library!)

M M M   m m m

Draw a line to match
the big M to the little m.

L   m

G

D   d

M   g

                     l

Color in the picture of the
thing that begins with M.

Find the M–word sticker so D.W. can see how marvelous she
looks in her muffler, hat, and mittens.

N N N   n n n

Draw a circle around the big N's in the sentence below. Draw a line underneath the little n's.

Noisy nurses

never need naps.

Draw a line to match the big N to the little n.

M   e

D   m

B   d

N   b

E   n

Fix the Neptunian newsman's sign.
Find the N–word sticker that will help.

Color in the objects below that do not begin with O.

In the sentence below, color the big O's in red. Color the little o's in blue.

Ollie Ostrich cooks only oatmeal cookies.

HELLO, ORION!

Our astronaut could use a healthy snack that begins with O.
Find the right sticker. (Hint: Its name is the same as its color.)

P P P P   p p p p

With a purple crayon, color in the fruit that begins with P.

Draw a line to match the big P and the little p.

C		e
P		b
B		c
G		p
E		g

PLANET PUZZLE

Find something to stick in the sky.
Then guess which planet this is.

Q Q Q   q q q

Color in the picture of the word that begins with Q.

Follow the small q's to find your way to the big Q.

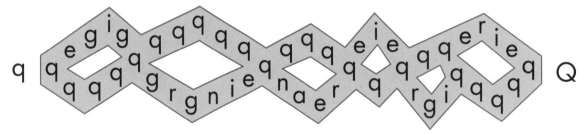

QUIET TIME

Question: Which coin begins with the letter Q?
Find the sticker and add it to Arthur's treasury.

R R R R   r r r r

With a red crayon, color in the picture of the word that begins with R.

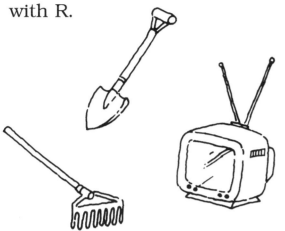

Color in the big R spaces with red.
Color in the little r spaces with green.

d	E	P	r	r	r	m	B	Q
n	e	C	f	r	q	G	H	n
O	I	j	R	R	R	N	k	C
a	K	R	B	m	i	R	F	b
G	c	R	L	A	o	R	J	g
B	h	P	R	R	R	D	I	M

ROBOT ROUND-UP

The astronauts need to measure the robots.
Can you find them the proper tool?

Make a ring around the object below that does not begin with the letter S.

Follow the s's to find your way through this really tiny maze.

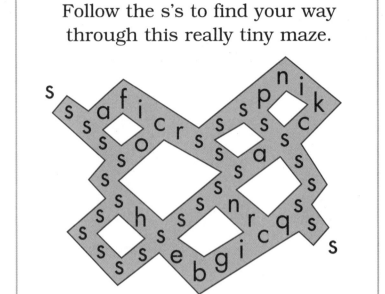

SWINGING ON A STAR

Arthur and D.W. are missing something. Find the S–word sticker and stick it on. Make it *sssssnappy!*

Take a crayon and cross three little t's. Now cross three big T's.

Color in the picture of the word that begins with T.

Terrible traffic! D.W., Arthur, and their alien friend are in trouble.
Find the sticker that proves it.

U U U   u u u

V V V   v v v

Draw a circle around the small u's. Draw a line beneath the big V's.

V u v U V u v U u

UPSIDE-DOWN VEHICLE

Unbelievable! Everything's upside down!
Find the U sticker, then find the V sticker.

W W W   W W W
X X X   X X X

Color in the pictures that begin with W.

Color in the picture that begins with X.

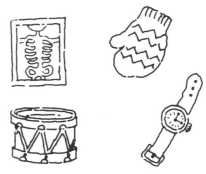

WOW! X MARKS THE SPOT

Y Y Y Y   y y y y
Z Z Z Z   z z z z

Draw a yellow circle around the picture that begins with Y.

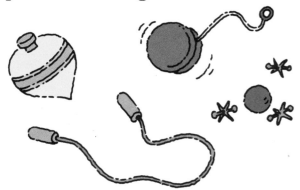

Draw an X through the thing that begins with Z.

Teaching is hard work! Arthur is fast asleep. D.W. needs something to get out of her astronaut suit. Help her.